# TIMELESS

## SHANE HEENAN

Timeless © Shane Heenan 2020

ISBN: 978-1-922460-29-5 (paperback)



Published in Australia by Shane Heenan and InHouse Publishing.
www.inhousepublishing.com.au

Printed in Australia by InHouse Print & Design.

# PART 1:

# JUST IN TIME

# Chapter 1

Before the fire, Jacob was a kid who was extremely social and always out with his friends, riding bikes and having sleepovers. Jacob had always had a slightly different perception to others, when things were not right. A sixth sense you could call it. An urge or feeling whenever he was in danger and the knack of suddenly finding himself in the right place at the right time, when others needed help.

As a young kid he had only had glimpses of this ability because … well … how many times would someone experience serious situations as a child? Narrowly missed accidents on his bike, and so on, were small glimpses of occasions when he continuously escaped unhurt. But nothing could have prepared him for what was to come.

One night, when he was twelve years old, he and his family were having dinner when the hairs on his arm stood up. Jacob had a feeling something was about going to happen but just couldn't work out what it was. Later that night Jacob asleep suddenly woke up with a start. He had a feeling that something terrible was going to happen. About ten minutes later, he realised that he could smell smoke. He walked out of his room into the lounge and found the entire room engulfed in flames. A later investigation found that the power point for the television had been faulty. It had sparked a fire on the carpet, which had spread to the drapes. Jacob desperately tried to get to his parents' room, but the flames enveloped the hallway and the only way out was the front door.

Jacob ran out into the street, screaming for help. The neighbours, seeing flames and smelling smoke, had called the emergency services, but by the time they arrived it was too late.

Jacob's parents had been quite wealthy. They had left him a large sum of money; however, Jacob knew nothing about this. Under the terms of the will he could not be told about it or access it until he was eighteen.

As he had no other family, social services placed him into foster care.

From this time on, Jacob became a very introverted young teen, although he was able to hone in on his 'gift' in order to feel and understand it. He remembered the night of the fire and made a quiet promise to himself that he would never let a situation get out of hand like that again.

Once Jacob was in his mid-teens he went out and got himself a job in a warehouse as a trainee storeman. He needed to get some money together to rent his own place because staying in a shared house just wasn't his thing at all. By the time he was in his late teens he was able to rent his own apartment.

When he was in his mid-twenties, he was clocking off from work one Friday afternoon, like any other day, when he came to an intersection with a green light. There was a black BMW in front of him, with a female driver. The traffic was moving at the speed limit of eighty kilometres per hour when a guy who was texting while driving ran the red light perpendicular to them. He was about to plough straight into the BMW. The driver saw him coming through her window and knew this could be the end for her.

Without a thought Jacob slammed down his foot on the accelerator to deliberately ram into the rear of her car, jolting her forward. Then, as he quickly slammed on his brakes, the offending car sped straight through, just shaving the rear of her car and the front of Jacob's vehicle.

Jacob sat there for a while in shock after he realised that his sixth sense had warned him again, but this time he had managed to save not only the driver of the BMW but also the driver who wasn't paying attention. Not a single person had a scratch on them. The only injury was to their shoulders, caused by their seat belts during the impact.

The woman stepped out of her car, shocked, at the same time Jacob did. He noticed how well dressed she was, as well as her dark hair that fell to her shoulders and her olive complexion. He couldn't help but think how gorgeous she was. She ran to him and hugged him, crying with joy.

"Thank you so much! What is your name?"

He replied, "You're welcome. My name is Jacob. What is yours?"

"I'm Hannah," she replied. "We will have to exchange numbers for insurance but I would also like to shout you out for a coffee sometime, if that would be okay? It's the least I could do. Please?"

Jacob accepted hesitantly. Normally he liked to keep to himself. After some discussion the two eventually decided to meet up at the Corner Café every second Friday afternoon for a coffee and if they felt like it, some drinks as well. Hannah chose this particular day as a reminder of the near miss they had both experienced and the day they had met.

# Chapter 2

Hannah had grown up in an outer Melbourne suburb of Toorak, a fairly wealthy area. However, her parents had gone through a breakup earlier in her life and her mother was looking after Hannah and her two sisters by herself, while trying to hold down a full-time job. As time went by, Hannah, being the eldest, had to help her mother to look after her two sisters. As a result, she developed leadership traits, so once she had completed year twelve at school she went straight into a business management course at university and prospered. Hannah had passed her course with flying colours and then taken up a job as general manager of a large freight forwarding company on the other side of town. Not wanting to let this opportunity go, she had moved out of home and found her own apartment in a suburb, not far from Essendon.

She took pride in always looking professional as anything less for her would not suffice. It was one afternoon while she was driving home and thinking about ways to improve her workplace that the near-miss incident had occurred. Hannah was in her late twenties when she met Jacob.

Over time their acquaintance turned into friendship and their friendship blossomed into a relationship.

One sunny Friday afternoon when the two met at the Corner Café, they were about to sit down at Jacob's favourite table near the window when Jacob suddenly had an urge to rather go down to the Tram Stop Café, a few blocks down the road. Hannah obliged as she thought that a change of scenery was just what they needed.

Once they arrived at the café Jacob opened the door for Hannah, as he often did. As he walked in, he noticed a roughly two-metre-long old tram track decorating the wall that looked as though it was hanging on by a thread. Only two nails seemed to be holding it in place. Jacob found this odd and thought that it must obviously be a piece of the old tram network. He also noticed plenty of old parts and accessories decorating the room, such as an old bag with coin dispenser that conductors had used to sell people their daily tickets. It was a very historic café and had round tables with four chairs per table.

Jacob turned to Hannah and said, "Let's sit over there in the corner by that tram track." Hannah was puzzled by this as Jacob always wanted to sit at the window and this corner table couldn't be any further from it. They both sat down and as they usually did, they began to talk about their day and just observe people going about their business. Jacob and Hannah noticed a tall, muscular gentleman in his mid-thirties walking through the doorway.

The man's name was Adrian. He was with his blonde-haired daughter, Kate, who looked about sixteen. Adrian and Kate came in and sat at the table right next to them.

# Chapter 3

Adrian had been brought up by two loving parents in a nice house not too far from Melbourne. They had brought him up with great values, and as he hit high school he had met the love of his life in Susan. They always went out together as often as they could. Once Adrian completed year ten, which was the minimum requirement, he left school to pursue his dream of becoming a fisherman.

Adrian had attended TAFE to get his certificate, which also allowed him to get a job offering him work experience in the field he was studying, which made it easier to get into fishing.

By the time he was no older than eighteen he had secured a job on the fishing vessel *Bountiful Lady* and began working a schedule of two weeks at sea, and two weeks off at home. Within a couple of years he had progressed from a deckhand who knew nothing to a leading deckhand on his vessel, and had become very proficient in what he did.

After one particular trip, he had come back to find Susan waiting for him at the dock with excitement on her face. Once the vessel was moored they had given each other a massive hug and kiss, as always, and Adrian had asked her, "What's going on? You look different."

She had answered, "I'm pregnant!" Adrian and Susan couldn't have been happier. For a long time Adrian had wanted them to have a child of their own. The couple wanted to find out the sex of the baby and when they found out it was a girl, they had both decided on the name Kate.

As Kate was growing up, Adrian had to keep working his two-week shifts on the trawler to make sure they had the money and security they needed. This made it hard on Susan, trying to cope with her own work and raising a child for essentially half the year by herself.

Every time Adrian came in to port there they would be, Susan and Kate, waiting for him at the docks and watching him come in. For Kate, it was always exciting to see her dad after he had been gone for so long. They would always go straight to a coffee shop to talk about how his trip was, how Susan was coping and, of course, what shenanigans Kate had gotten up to. This was their routine every time without fail and it was a highlight in Adrian's life.

On one trip, when Adrian was in his mid-thirties and Kate was in her mid-teens, the fishing vessel had had a major engine problem and had to be towed into port for repairs. Adrian hadn't let Susan know as he'd wanted to go home and surprise her.

When he arrived home, he saw an unfamiliar car in the driveway. He walked up to the door, unlocked it and walked in. He heard a moaning noise. He followed the noise to the bedroom, worrying that Susan might be sick or hurt, but found it was neither. She was with another guy in their bed.

Adrian was furious. Trying to keep a level head, he had ordered them both to leave. Susan had desperately tried to explain herself. Really though, how could she have explained it to a person with values such as his?

Adrian had packed what he could and moved into his own apartment. He knew he had to stay friends with Susan for Kate's sake, which really was what it was all about for him. Since Kate was in her mid-teens they were able to talk to her as candidly as possible, without giving too many details. Adrian had asked one thing of Susan: to go to the wharf with Kate after every trip. Susan, of course, said yes to this request for two reasons: one, because she had caused the breakup, and two, so that Kate could still see her dad come into port, which was her favourite thing to do.

About a year later Adrian came into port again and Susan and Kate were both there waiting for him, as Susan had promised. Once moored, he jumped over the gunnel to the wharf and gave Kate a big hug and kiss. He also gave Susan a peck on the check, as they believed they should still show some form of affection in front of Kate. Adrian turned to Kate and said, "Would you like to catch a tram to a different coffee shop this time? I feel like being around people because it gets lonely out there with no land in sight and minimal crew."

Kate happily obliged, saying, "Yeah, Dad, that would be awesome. I want to hear everything you did this season." And Adrian turned to her saying, "I have a big story for you from this trip, Kate!"

While they were on their tram ride they were thinking of places to go when Kate said, "Let's go to the Tram Stop Café in Essendon. It's got a lot of people so I think you would love it." She smiled and Adrian nodded in agreement, with excited eyes.

As they walked into the café Adrian asked Kate, "Would you like to hear the scary story about what happened to me this trip?"

Kate replied, "For sure, Dad. Give me your best!"

Adrian said, "Well, this is definitely it. So, while we were steaming to another location to see if we could get a bigger catch I was ordered by the skipper to run out on the boom and down to the boards to change over a shackle. It was night time and we were steaming full throttle, side-on to the weather, and while I was on the boards I noticed I had gone extremely high up. And so I looked at the boom on the other side of the boat and realised that we had hit a big wave and half of the other boom was in the water! Now Kate, basic physics says that what goes up must come down, right? I realised that I was gonna go down too, and sure enough my side started to come down. I had no time to react so I just leapt up from the boards and reached for the wire going across the booms that held the boards up. Thank God I did, because the boom went underwater and took me with it! Like I said, it was full throttle so it was hard holding on, while getting dragged through the water. The boat finally rolled the other way and I came up out of the water. It must have been adrenaline, but I was able to pull myself up onto the boom, just from the trawl wire. Then I heard the boat slowing down.

"Luckily the boys were watching me and let my skipper know what had happened, and I don't think they said it nicely to him, either. Because you see, Kate, the ocean is a massive place and to find someone in it at night is near impossible. I walked back down the boom and the guys put a towel around me and sat me in the galley. I think I was in severe shock."

Adrian's daughter was hanging off every word he was saying because she always missed her dad when he was away and loved him very much. Needless to say, his adventures weren't small ones either and this story was no exception.

At the next table, Jacob and Hannah couldn't help but listen in on Adrian's tales and were amazed to hear about what happens in the life of a fisherman.

Suddenly they heard screeching tyres outside the café. An out-of-control car was headed straight for the café. In fact, it was headed straight for them.

It smashed through the large glass windows. Without a thought, Jacob kicked the wall where the rail was sitting. The rail was heavy and the nails were weak, so the nails gave way instantly and the rail fell quickly. Jacob jammed the end closest to him into the bottom corner of the room while the other end hung in the air – just in time for the front of the car to jam into it at speed, which catapulted the car into the air, where it sat, with the wheels spinning furiously, right next to Kate's head. Jacob had just saved their lives.

Instantly, Jacob told Adrian and Kate, "We need to go now. Trust me; we don't want to be around when the police show up and ask endless questions, as I've seen that you two have only a short amount of time to spend together."

With that, they all left immediately. They jumped into Jacob's car and he took them all back to his place.

Meanwhile the police did show up and began getting statements from the customers and workers. Suddenly two Australian Secret Intelligence Service, or ASIS, agents dressed in suits arrived at the scene, introducing themselves as Tillerson and Greenwood. One police officer said to them, "This is a bit below your pay grade, isn't it?" Agent Tillerson responded, "Things that are below our pay grade sometimes turn out to be much bigger than expected."

The agents took a description of the man who had pulled off this miracle to keep on file in case anything like this should ever happen again.

And so it was that on a Friday afternoon, Jacob, Hannah, Adrian and Kate were all sitting in Jacob's kitchen having a beer, and a coke for Kate, reminiscing on the events that had just transpired. Adrian turned to Jacob and said, "I am forever in your debt. You saved us both and I assure you I will always be on call if ever you need help."

Jacob and Hannah drove Adrian and Kate to the train station so they could make their way home. On the way, Adrian and Jacob exchanged phone numbers and swore to keep in contact. A month later, due to

Adrian's work schedule, the fortnightly Friday afternoon catch-ups now had a new member.

Adrian, true to his word, turned up at 5.00 pm the next Friday. He was dressed to impress in a buttoned-up shirt and jeans, with his hair slicked back, as he was nervous and excited about seeing them again. Jacob and Hannah had just chosen a table in the front of the Corner Café when Hannah spotted Adrian walking through the front doorway. Hannah stood with a great big smile, her olive complexion making her white teeth glow even brighter. "Oh my God, it's so good to see you. How are you and Kate doing?" she exclaimed. Adrian replied, "Kate is fine – thanks to you, Jacob." He nodded at Jacob.

"These last two weeks away have felt like a long time. I have had close calls out at sea, but last time we met was crazy!" he exclaimed. After a couple of coffees they headed back to Jacob's apartment for a few beers and called it a night. As Adrian was leaving he said, "I won't be able to make your fortnightly coffee but if I could join you monthly that would be terrific."

Jacob replied, "You just tell us when you're available and it'll be done," which Hannah wholeheartedly agreed to.

# Chapter 4

Jacob received a call one month later from Adrian wanting to catch up over a coffee on their usual Friday afternoon at the Corner Café, which Jacob of course wanted to do, so they all met up again. As they all approached the usual table by the window Jacob stopped walking and said, "I feel like a bit of fun, guys. Let's have a coffee and then go somewhere different. What do you think?"

Adrian and Hannah both looked at each other with uncertainty and Hannah said, "I don't know if that's such a great idea, given your history of changing places, buddy!" which both Adrian and Hannah chuckled about.

However, Jacob was very firm about this feeling and said in a serious tone, "Let's go and see a band or something! I will make you a deal. You guys come with me and I will drive."

Reluctantly they both accepted his request and after a coffee headed down to the Royal Hotel, which was no further than a ten-minute drive from the Corner Café. When they arrived at the hotel, they walked straight into the bar and ordered a drink each – a Stella Artois for Jacob, a Carlton Draught for Adrian and a glass of champagne for Hannah.

Jacob, as usual, chose a table near the window. It was directly in front of the band, which was playing rock music from the '80s and '90s. They enjoyed watching people boogie on the dance floor and couldn't help but notice an Arabian-looking fellow in his mid-twenties with thick, scruffy black hair and a beard that had been shaved deliberately to stubble. He was ripping it up on the dance floor. He had a big smile and was asking various girls to dance. They heard him say his name was Dhillion.

When Dhillion was younger, his parents had held very strict Arabic views. However, they had come to Australia for their son to hopefully have a more fulfilling life so they really never pushed their beliefs onto him but taught him to respect the belief of others, which he always did. As a result, Dhillion grew up with a mind that was open to all possibilities. He became a very intelligent boy at school who soon focused his attention on computers. He always enjoyed math and science, but computers were the icing on the cake for him.

Once he had finished year twelve at high school he went straight to university where he studied computer science and internet technology, or 'IT'. He passed these courses with flying colours and went on to get a job at a very well-established company. Dhillion moved out as soon as he had finished his degree. Although he already had two computers at home, he wanted more. He enjoyed pushing himself to limits that other people wouldn't normally go to, due to his passion for computers, science and math, but he also loved to have fun. He had a passion for music as well, so whenever he was on the computer he found that playing his favourite tracks through headphones helped him concentrate. Having a love for music meant he loved to dance and he did that as often as he could, so, at home, he always kept his computer room door closed. The rest of the house was always tidy, not just for his parents' visits, but more so for the woman he hoped to bring home one day.

Dhillion loved to play matchmaker for people as well, so when he met a guy called Evan at the Royal Hotel, he just had to intervene and offer his advice.

An hour or so later, both Dhillion and Evan were dancing right on the outer edge of the dance floor, which wasn't too far from Jacob, Adrian and Hannah, when they all heard a faint cracking noise coming from the ceiling.

They all looked up, and then an almighty crack sounded and the ceiling plaster gave way. Jacob, being the closest to the pair of guys dancing, leapt from his seat and pushed both Dhillion and Evan out of the way while diving to his right as the plaster fell, just missing them all by millimetres. The band instantly stopped playing. The lead singer had just witnessed the whole event transpire. He was baffled that no one was hurt and at what Jacob had done. It seemed unreal to him.

Evan stood up and said, "Praise God! You just saved my life!" and hugged Jacob.

With that, Dhillion stood up and said, "Yes. Thank you for saving us."

Jacob reassured them and then said, "We need to go now. Or would you like to spend the rest of your night with the police, answering questions?"

Evan shook his head furiously and said, "No way. Where do we go?" Jacob told them to jump into his car and suggested he take them back to his apartment for a couple of beers, which would become the beginning of Dhillion and Evan joining their regular Friday night meetings.

Just after they had left, sure enough, the police turned up. While they were interviewing people, Agents Tillerson and Greenwood turned up again. They walked straight to the officer in charge and requested to speak to the main witness. As the lead singer had seen the whole thing transpire, he was the obvious choice to interview. He gave a very descriptive portrait of the man who had saved Evan and Dhillion and described what he had actually done to save them. Agents Tillerson and Greenwood began to realise that this was a pattern. It was the same person from previous accidents. This guy was always there – at the right time and in the right place. Agents Tillerson and Greenwood had much bigger plans for Jacob now that they could see that he was definitely a worthy candidate for what they had in store for him. Their plan was to discover just how far he could go in any given situation and how many people he could save.

They both headed back to base to tell their boss about Jacob and to get approval to go ahead with their plan.

# Chapter 5

One Thursday morning Jacob was sitting by himself in his apartment reading a book and drinking his coffee before work, as he always did, when he got a sudden urge to leave. He stood up and began walking to the door. He reached for the handle and then stopped. He thought, *I can't keep doing this.* And so he turned around and sat back down to keep drinking his coffee and reading his book. But he was very agitated. He didn't realise that this time the urge was to save himself, no one else.

Jacob's house was suddenly surrounded by police and about fifty SWAT officers, accompanied by Agents Tillerson and Greenwood. That was when Jacob realised he should have left when he had had the chance. Now he had no choice but to leave with the agents. They forced him into a car and took him to an abandoned warehouse about fifty kilometres away. But this was no ordinary warehouse. It seemed abandoned from the front, but once they walked inside Jacob thought, *Holy shit! This place is completely decked out!* He kept asking the agents, "What's going on?" but there was no answer, as they sat him down and strapped his wrists and legs to the chair.

They hooked him up to monitors to keep an eye on his blood pressure and adrenalin, but also put him on a drip. They then proceeded to put a strange-looking helmet with wires coming from it on his head. They injected him with a sleeping solution to create in his mind a dreamlike simulation of reality.

This simulation system was originally created to emulate complex human activity in urban environments that featured autonomous virtual pedestrians, such as crowd simulations for bombings. They then began experimenting with the idea of putting human consciousness into the simulation. They had succeeded after many trials. However, the simulations started small: five to ten minutes with a three-hour break, then twenty to thirty minutes with a five-hour break, as the subject's mind was unable to survive long periods of time in the simulation straight away. The brain needed to be eased into it and when the subject (in this case, Jacob) was ejected from the simulation the world around him began to get ripped away slowly and became a white tunnel that got smaller and smaller until he was in complete darkness and fully asleep again.

They proceeded to run all types of simulations on Jacob, from car accidents on a freeway to an avalanche on a bushwalk. They even tried bomb explosions near to where he was standing and a crowd crush at a soccer stadium, to test whether his 'urge' would take him away from the situation.

They eventually discovered that he couldn't save everyone around him (although he tried his best to do so). If bystanders were in his vicinity he had a higher chance of saving them, but always found a way out himself.

# Chapter 6

While Jacob was being tested in these different scenarios in the simulation, Hannah, Adrian, Dhillion and Evan had no idea what was happening. They were all waiting for their call from Jacob for their usual Friday meeting. But the call never came.

They became concerned so they all decided to meet at Jacob's apartment. Once they walked through the front doorway they were shocked to see such a mess. Things just appeared to have been thrown around and the whole place was upside down. They grabbed a chair each and sat down to discuss first of all where he could be, and second, what they could do. Hannah said, "I'm so worried, guys. We need to find him!"

Adrian replied, "Yes, we need to find him. What if we call all the hospitals in the area? He might be in one of them."

Then Evan said, "Yes, let's do that, but don't call the police. You know how he doesn't like to get involved with the police."

"If we can't find him in the hospitals then let me have a go at finding him," Dhillion said. He had a wry smile as he looked at the computer but they didn't have time to worry about what he was thinking right now.

Hannah stood up and said, "Right! Let's look up every single hospital and we'll nominate a hospital each to call."

After many calls, they still had no luck in finding Jacob. Dhillion had had enough and said, "My turn, guys! We need to go to my place. I have the equipment we need to search for him properly."

On their way to Dhillion's, Evan began to pray. "Dear God, please help us find our friend and bring him back to us safely." Adrian turned around and said, "I hope he heard you, brother!"

They had never been to Dhillion's house before, so when they arrived, they all thought it looked rather nice. It was a townhouse with a brick façade and looked very new. Hannah said, "Oh, this looks gorgeous, Dhil!"

He replied, "You haven't seen anything yet, darlin'," as he smiled a secretive smile.

They all walked up to the front of the house while Dhillion unlocked the door. Everyone was keen to look inside as Dhillion opened the door, but Adrian just could not wait. He easily brushed Dhillion aside as if he were a kid who wanted to be the first into a games room and walked inside as the others followed.

It was a clean and tidy house, Adrian thought, as he noticed the flowers sitting on the hallway table. Hannah couldn't help herself and had to smell them. "Fake!" she said, after a brief sniff. "These flowers are fake."

Dhillion had a chuckle at this and said, "Do you think I could keep those things alive if they were real? I don't have time for that nonsense." As Dhillion was saying this, Evan walked up to a door, thinking, *I wonder what else he gets up to! That smile he gave earlier seemed a little bit suspect.*

As Dhillion walked through the doorway into a bedroom he swung around to Evan and said, "This, my friend, is why we are here."

Evan glanced inside, opening the door slowly, and muttered quietly, "What the hell is this?" Adrian and Hannah knew something had to be going on in the bedroom for Evan to say something like that. Dhillion stood there with a straight back and a big smile, and with what appeared to be a lot of pride, as they all walked in. The room was full of electronics. Five computers, all with their own keyboard and mouse, were lined up in a half circle, each fronted by a black leather chair on wheels. They noticed that the size of the computer modem was enormous, with wires coming out of it in all directions. It had just about everything you could think of for a supersized computer system.

Hannah's jaw dropped as she turned to Dhillion and said, "What do you do for work again, Dhil?"

He replied, "I'm a computer programmer."

Hannah stood there with questioning eyes and said, "This is a bit of overkill, isn't it?"

Dhillion replied, "It would seem that way to you, I suppose, Hannah, but this is my hobby. This is what I do outside of work during the week, or when I'm not out having fun."

Adrian then said, "What in God's name is your hobby?" as he looked around the room.

Dhillion replied, "Well ... I kind of like to hack other systems. But not small ones. Systems that are extraordinarily hard to decipher. Government systems."

Hannah was speechless, like the rest of them, when Dhillion jumped into his chair and pressed a key on each keyboard to start up the fun. He went to the middle screen and opened up a program which just said, 'Enter number here'. So Dhillion pulled out his phone, typed in Jacob's number and clicked 'Enter'. The screen turned into an aerial-view map with a red dot in the middle of it. It began searching. All of a sudden it stopped searching and zoomed in on an industrial estate and said, 'Phone found'.

Hannah yelled, "We found him!" and hugged the closest person, who was Adrian.

Dhillion had to halt the celebration by saying, "Hold on a minute, guys," as he opened up another screen on the left and searched the address that was given so he could have a good look at the building. Once he had a panoramic view of the building he said, "I've seen this building before in some files I hacked and it wasn't in a public forum, either. I reckon this isn't just an abandoned warehouse and from memory, this was actually something top secret."

Dhillion then opened up a computer on the right-hand side, typed in a couple of codes and then the address of the building, and clicked 'Search'. Not thirty seconds later it read, 'New simulation facility'. Then it started scrolling through what would look like jargon to most people but Dhillion knew better. He turned to them with his eyes wide and said, "Holy shit!"

They all started asking, "What, Dhillion? What is it? Tell us!"

Dhillion replied, "To put it simply, they created a simulation of our perceived world into a computer. It was originally only for testing human responses to emergency situations but they have seriously upgraded this system to actually be capable of inserting a human into the system in a dreamlike state. From what I can see here, they start off with the patient (and in this case I would say, Jacob) in the simulation for five to ten minutes with a three-hour break, then for twenty to thirty minutes with a five-hour break, and so on and so on. They put him to sleep in the real world so it would seem to Jacob that it was a dream, and that's all." Also – one more issue, guys. If he is in the simulation when we get there, then there is only one way for him to wake up out of it. He has to jump from a high position to his death, which will jolt him out."

Hannah turned around and said, "Wait, wait, wait! Are you telling me agents kidnapped Jacob and put him into a computer? Is that what you're saying?"

"Yes. Unfortunately yes," Dhillion replied.

Adrian turned to Evan and then back to Dhillion and asked, "So … what can we do to get him back?"

Dhillion started scrolling through the information download on the computer and said, "Well, it seems they have control over the surveillance cameras, plus a few of their own, in and around a five-hundred-metre radius of the building. Most have motion sensors so I will need my laptop at least to keep tabs on that and also, we will have to tap into the simulation as well. I don't think I can make us visible but I could get us in so we can talk to him. I dare say it would be like someone is talking to you but they are everywhere and nowhere. Then we can tell him what to do."

Hannah then said, "Right. Dhillion – you get everything ready for that and we will all go home and get some sleep because tomorrow will be an interesting day – a Saturday that will be a little different for us all. Let's meet up at Jacob's at 7.00 am."

Evan turned to Hannah and said, "Maybe you should dress down for tomorrow? You can't really run with high heels!"

They both giggled at that. Then Hannah replied, "Evan … maybe a good prayer is in order for us and Jacob tonight."

Evan nodded. "I'm all over that part, Hannah!" And with that, they all went their separate ways.

Soon it was 7.00 am and they were all together at Jacob's house. They all hopped into Evan's car and set off to the abandoned warehouse. Evan had been a dedicated Christian who helped people by picking them up from their homes, bringing them to church and then driving them home, so his SUV and driving skills were more than acceptable for this mission.

Once they were within a kilometre of the building they all had to hop out and start walking. Adrian had brought walkie-talkies to allow them all to communicate, because Dhillion would have to stay in the car with Evan. It was his job to hack into the surveillance system and the simulation: a massive job in itself.

When Hannah and Adrian got to the five-hundred-metre radius where the cameras were situated, Adrian pulled out his walkie-talkie and asked Dhillion, "Are the cameras off?"

Dhillion replied, "Not all of them, champ. For the first hundred metres you're by yourself, I'm afraid. I have shut down the rest within four hundred metres."

Adrian then said to Hannah, "Let's go through the back of that shop."

As they entered, they saw a motion-detection camera in the top corner of the shop so they pushed a chair across the room and with that, the camera moved with the chair. They dashed through the shop, just barely making it out without the camera seeing them.

Hannah jumped on the walkie-talkie and said, "Are the cameras down from here?"

Dhillion replied, "Yes, they sure are." So they ran until they got to the warehouse. Dhillion had told them to let him know when they got there and then told them to wait around the side of the warehouse until he said otherwise.

Dhillion then sent a message through his computer to the agents holding Jacob saying, 'Agents to go directly to base for emergency meeting'. The agents had no choice but to leave and follow the directions given to them.

As Hannah and Adrian began to run into the building, Dhillion's voice came over the walkie-talkie saying, "They seem to have him on a longer simulation this time. He is in a hospital, in a wheelchair and paralysed! I think they are trying to see if he can cure himself! Okay, Hannah, you guys need to be next to him when he wakes up to unplug everything as he will be disorientated. You guys may need to carry him out of there, and quickly! I'm sending the message to him now."

Dhillion then picked up his headset, placed it over his head and then pressed 'Enter' on his laptop.

"Jacob," he announced in the simulation.

This shocked Jacob and he started frantically looking around in his wheelchair. "Who is that?" Jacob exclaimed.

"Jacob, this is Dhillion and unfortunately you can't see me but I have some bad news for you. You're in a simulation. Agents captured you, put you to sleep and hooked you up to the machine."

Jacob replied, "How do I get out?"

Dhillion replied, "You won't like this but you need to jump from a great height to what will feel like your death. This is the only way to produce enough adrenaline to wake you out of this dream and bring you back to reality. Hannah and Adrian are there waiting for you."

"They came too?" Jacob asked.

"Yes, of course they did. Evan is here with me too," replied Dhillion.

So Jacob rolled down the hallway and into a lift. He went up to the sixth floor and went to a window. He opened it and pulled himself onto the ledge saying, "Are you sure about this?"

Dhillion said, "Yes, and you need to jump now before the agents come back!" Jacob jumped and was screaming all the way down in terror until there was a huge *thump*. He hit the concrete and then woke up with Hannah and Adrian by his side.

They quickly unhooked him and Adrian piggybacked Jacob out of there while Hannah grabbed Jacob's phone that was sitting nearby and placed it in his jacket pocket. Once they got to the front of the warehouse

Evan and Dhillion were in the car waiting for them. They all quickly got into the car and went straight to Jacob's house. On the way, they discussed what to do next. In the car, Jacob, still very groggy, took his jacket off, which still had his phone in the pocket, and put it at his feet saying, "I need to get away from here! They will just come back for me. They know where I live now."

Hannah stroked his hair and said, "I will come with you."

"No! You have a life here, an apartment and a career and I don't want you giving everything up for me," Jacob exclaimed.

Hannah then replied, "I will give up whatever I like because it's mine and I will give it up for you!"

With that, Dhillion said, with his usual wry smile, "I will make the necessary adjustments."

Evan said, "Once we are at your place you need to grab as much as possible and get the hell outta there!"

Jacob then said, "There is only one thing I need from there."

When they arrived, Jacob stepped out of the car and tentatively walked to the front door with Hannah by his side. Hannah opened the door and let him in and he walked straight to his bedroom closet where he reached up and grabbed a shoe box. "What's in there?" Hannah asked.

"Just old photos and letters from my parents when I was young, before the fire." A flashback of the funeral played through his head.

"Okay. Let's go!" Hannah said.

"Where to?" Jacob asked, with a look of confusion on his face.

Hannah replied, "To Dhillion's place for now and we can go from there. Like Dhil said, he can make the adjustments."

With that, they quickly walked to the car and stepped inside. Adrian said, "Is that it? A shoe box?"

Jacob smiled and Dhillion told Evan, "Let's go, brother. Drive to my place as quickly as possible without bringing any attention to us."

Once they got to Dhillion's house they walked through the front door and Jacob went to smell the flowers in the hallway. Hannah quickly stopped him and said, "No, honey, they are fake. I did the same thing." Adrian and Evan couldn't help but laugh at this.

Dhillion told everyone to wait in the dining room for him as he had some work to do. It was no later than fifteen minutes when Dhillion came back with a stack of things in his hands. He went straight to Jacob and handed them to him, one by one, explaining what they were.

"Here is your new identity, Jacob. You will now be moving to tropical Cairns in Queensland. You have a new passport, tax file number, bank account and … oh, yeah … your new name is Jake Redpath. I hope you're happy with that. I tried to keep it as close to your real name as possible, but different enough to keep you under the radar. I could've given you the name Dhillion but you know … there can be only one!" And with that, they all had a chuckle but their smiles slowly turned to seriousness as Dhillion said, "I want us to still keep in contact and meet if we can. I will miss you, both of you," looking at Hannah as well.

So they all said their goodbyes and Hannah and Jacob went to the car. They drove straight to her apartment where she said, "I've just got to grab a few things like clothes, makeup and shoes. I don't need anything else from there and I can organise everything else from Queensland."

After about thirty minutes they set off on their long trip. The jacket with Jacob's phone in the pocket was still on the floor at the back, amongst Hannah's clothes. Hannah said, "We will always make time to see them. They are true friends who will obviously always be there."

Jacob said, "I know, and we will always be in touch." They pulled into a service station and once Jacob had finished fuelling up the car, he walked inside to pay for it while Hannah sat in the car waiting. Behind her, a nice black Ford Territory SUV had pulled up, apparently waiting to fuel up as well. But what neither Hannah nor Jacob noticed was a man hopping out of the SUV, walking to the back of their car, placing a tracking device under the rear bumper of the car and then calmly walking back to his car. Jacob and Hannah set off happily to start their new life together.

As they pulled over four hours later to stretch their legs, Jacob did a walkaround of the car to check the tires. When he got to the rear of the car, he noticed that there was a faint flashing red light coming from under the bumper and found the device. He asked Hannah what she thought it was but she had no idea, so he threw it into the bin and they carried on without another thought.

# PART 2:

# OUT OF TIME

# Chapter 7

In order to escape the agents hunting them down, Dhillion had organised for both Jacob and Hannah to live far away in Cairns.

On the way to their destination they discovered many places to explore on overnight stays. Sometimes they even stayed two nights to have a look around, if they really liked where they were. Airlie Beach seemed like a beautiful place to them: clear water on the beach, a harbour and palm trees aplenty – a small taste of what was to come. They both decided to stay there for two nights, due to its beauty.

On the second day Hannah did a bit of window shopping while Jacob walked down to the harbour to admire all of the boats. He thought of his friend, Adrian, who had spent so much of his life at sea. This naturally flowed on to thoughts of all his friends.

Hannah had found a gorgeous Airlie Beach bangle that she wanted to buy. She tried calling Jacob on his phone to hear his thoughts, as the bracelet was quite expensive, but the phone just kept ringing and going to voicemail. Hannah became concerned because Jacob always answered his phone.

Some hours later they both joined up again and Hannah asked Jacob why he hadn't answered his phone. He pulled out the new phone Dhillion had arranged for him and went through his recent call list. It wasn't very long, and there was no missed call from Hannah.

Then Jacob had a thought and said, "Which phone did you call, babe?" Even as he was saying it, he grabbed Hannah's phone and had a look in her list of recent calls. When he saw his old number his jaw dropped.

"Do you realise you called my old phone? Did it actually ring?"

Hannah replied, "Yes, it did and it even went to your voicemail. Sorry, babe, I just did it out of habit, I think."

Jacob then asked Hannah, "But why do you still have the number? Wasn't the phone left with the agents back at the warehouse? Let's go to the car and try one more time and see if the phone rings."

Once they were back at the car Hannah called again. Jacob heard the phone ringing.

"Holy shit!" he said. "It's here! How can it be here?"

He started digging through Hannah's clothes that were lumped together on the back seat of the car and came across his old jacket. He had a flashback of being taken out to the car, and of taking the jacket off and throwing it on the floor.

"You brought it with us?" Jacob asked. With a look of shock on her face Hannah replied, "I'm so sorry, Jacob – I forgot all about it!"

"Do you realise they can track this, babe?" Jacob said. "Just like Dhillion tracked it to find me. They are probably following us right now!" And with that, he threw the phone as hard as he could onto the concrete path and began jumping on it until it was in pieces. He then picked it all up and threw it in the bin.

"Let's hope we lose them from here and thank God we found it now and not at our new house. We are halfway up the coast of Queensland so they don't have to look too far if they are following us, which I'm sure they are."

Hannah began crying, with her hands over her face, so Jacob gave her a big hug, wiped her tears away and gave her a tender kiss. They both agreed to carry on to Cairns sooner rather than later, in light of this new problem. They also agreed to drive the rest of the way nonstop so they could hopefully lose the agents that were possibly following them.

# Chapter 8

Once they came close to Cairns they typed the address they were given by Dhillion into the GPS: '24 Cover Street, Kewarra Beach'. They found it was forty-five minutes past Cairns, which excited them both because they knew that the further north they went, the more breathtaking the scenery would become.

As they drove into the suburb they looked at each other with big smiles on their faces. They had arrived at a beautifully quiet suburb that had palm trees everywhere they looked, with the constant smell of the ocean in a lightly salted breeze. As they drove up to the house they couldn't believe it.

"A Queenslander!" Jacob yelled in excitement.

Hannah asked Jacob what a Queenslander was, and Jacob told her that they were houses built on stilts to handle floods and cyclones.

Hannah and Jacob grabbed a bag each from the boot of the car and headed up the stairs, which were located on the right-hand side of the house. They found a note on the door: 'Attention Jacob – Welcome to your new home. Your keys are in the electrical box and I hope that you enjoy this house that I have chosen for you. From your friend, Dhillion'.

As Hannah and Jacob walked inside they couldn't believe what they were seeing. It was luxury all the way, including leather couches, a big-screen television, a ducted cooling system and a veranda that seemed to encompass the house. Everything they needed for a new life together.

Once they had unpacked what they had brought in the SUV, they both sat down with a coffee and began looking for work. Hannah had already called to ensure her life in Melbourne had been completely wrapped up.

Two days later, Jacob and Hannah were walking along the beach admiring the view of the calm clear water and the palm trees, when suddenly, Jacob heard a young girl's voice cry out, "Help! Help! Help!"

He looked around anxiously. Hannah asked, "What are you looking for?"

"Don't you hear that? It sounds like a girl is in trouble," said Jacob.

"No," Hannah replied, "I don't hear a thing."

# Chapter 9

Meanwhile, Agents Tillerson and Greenwood had arrived in Airlie Beach, where Jacob's old phone was last active. They walked straight up to the exact bin it had been thrown into and looked at each other.

Tillerson said, "They can't be far away, Greenwood. I'm sure they are long gone. Since they took the trouble to destroy the phone, they are probably aware of us by now. However, let's have a look around."

Agent Greenwood replied, "I will have a look at the harbour and speak to some people. Who knows? We might get lucky."

Agent Greenwood took out a photo of Jacob and asked around the harbour whether anyone had spotted a man who looked similar. An older couple said they believed they had, but they weren't really sure. It appeared no one had actually spoken with them.

However, Agent Tillerson had more luck. He was walking through the strip of shops and came across a gift shop. When he asked the lady behind the counter if she had seen the man in the photo, she replied, "Yes, I did see him, and he was with a young lady."

The agent collected all the information he could on the lady as well, and with that, both agents met up again. They told each other of their encounters, and Tillerson said, "They aren't here but we know they were. We can't go back to base until we find them. I think we should move further north because that's the way they've been headed so far. We'll stop at each town and keep asking around. They can only go so far."

Greenwood agreed. They jumped into their car and headed north.

# Chapter 10

Jacob and Hannah were on the beach in Cairns. They were relaxing after a cool swim when Jacob spotted a woman reading a book and sunbathing on a large beach towel. In his ears, he suddenly heard a cry for help. He looked out over the water, where he could see splashing.

"Oh my God! Look there, babe," he cried, his arm outstretched and his finger pointing into the distance. "I think she is in trouble!"

He started to run towards the girl in the water.

"How do you know it's a girl?" Hannah asked. "What the hell is going on?"

Jacob was already diving into the water. He was able to reach her quickly, as she wasn't very far out. He saw that she looked no older than twelve.

The mother dropped her book when she noticed Jacob running towards her daughter.

"Oh, no!" she whispered, as she watched Jacob pull the girl out coughing and spluttering. She ran down to her daughter.

Jacob was holding the young girl's back up with one hand, encouraging her to keep coughing to clear her airways, while she was sitting on the sand. Her mum arrived and hugged her, saying, "Oh my God, Tahlia! Are you okay, honey?"

She then turned her attention to Jacob who had Hannah by his side and said, "Thank you so much! You saved my daughter's life. How can I possibly repay you?"

Jacob replied, "It's fine. She is alright and that's all that matters, but please, I don't mean to be rude, but you need to keep a close eye on her while she is in the water. My name is Jacob and this gorgeous woman next to me is Hannah. I know your daughter's name, but what is yours?"

"My name is Jane," she replied, and with that, Jacob stood up and brushed the sand off himself. He was dripping wet; however, the humid warmth would dry him quickly.

Both Hannah and Jacob told Jane that they hoped to meet under better circumstances next time, and said goodbye to her and Tahlia.

As Jacob and Hannah began walking back towards the car, Hannah asked Jacob, "How did you know? I mean, I get that you heard her but seriously, my hearing is great and I didn't hear a thing."

Jacob replied, "It was just ear-piercing! I don't understand it either. Maybe I have a super hearing ability!" He said it with a chuckle.

Hannah smiled at this but was wondering at the same time whether there may have been something to it, because both of their versions of events were starkly different. Jacob's was that the sound had been ear-piercing. But she hadn't heard it at all.

# Chapter 11

By now both Jacob and Hannah had found jobs in Cairns. The hours were from 8.30 am to 5.00 pm, Monday to Friday, which suited them both to a tee. Jacob had found a warehouse storeman's job again, which he had always enjoyed doing, and Hannah had found a managerial job for a freight forwarding company, which was very similar to what she had been doing in Melbourne.

Two weeks after their encounter with Tahlia and Jane, on a Thursday afternoon, Jacob had the sudden feeling that he should leave. Friday was a public holiday, so he decided to leave work early and head home. As he was driving home on the outskirts of Cairns, a massive shiver passed right through his whole body, and he had no idea why. He didn't think much of it.

But at exactly the same time, agents Tillerson and Greenwood were driving past on the opposite side of the road. Although he was unaware of it, Jacob's intuition or sixth sense was getting stronger.

On his drive home he noticed a jewellery shop in the middle of a strip of shops and decided to go in for a quick look. He had been pondering popping the question to Hannah.

He asked the woman behind the counter if she could help him by showing him a ring with a diamond. She brought out a beautiful white gold ring with a sparkling diamond. Jacob was taken with it immediately.

"Could I please buy that one?" he asked. The woman behind the counter replied, "Yes, of course. It is lovely. Do you have her ring size?"

Jacob had no idea so he just guessed a size and hoped for the best – risky business, but it was the only way for him to get it without Hannah knowing.

Once Jacob had bought the ring he left with a terrific sense of accomplishment and excitement, and so, on his way home, he decided to stop at a local pub to have a beer and hopefully talk about the AFL and what chances his beloved team, Richmond Tigers, had of making the finals.

While in discussion with a local man named Rob, their conversation drifted from talking about footy to the beauty of the landscape in North Queensland and Rob began telling Jacob that the Daintree Rainforest was a spectacular place and should be seen, just as the Great Barrier Reef should be seen. Rob began rattling off names like Kuranda, Malanda Falls and others, but Kuranda sounded amazing to Jacob as it had markets, lookouts and waterfalls.

Jacob thanked Rob for the advice, finished his beer and said his farewell as it was time to head home. He had the ring in his pocket and a place in mind where he wanted to propose to Hannah.

Once Jacob arrived home he told Hannah of the conversation he had had with Rob and asked her if she would be interested in going to Kuranda. Hannah was quite excited by the idea and wanted to go the following morning.

# Chapter 12

Not long after their decision to go to Kuranda, Jacob received a call from Dhillion. He was smiling from ear to ear to hear from his good friend. However, this would not be the kind of call Jacob was expecting.

Jacob answered the phone and said, "Dhillion! How are you, buddy? What's been happening?" and Dhillion replied, "I'm well, mate. I have been keeping busy and I have heaps to tell you but unfortunately I'm calling to give you some bad news."

Jacob's smile started to disappear when he asked Dhillion, "Why? What's happened?"

Dhillion replied, "I've been keeping an eye on these agents online, mate, and they have been tracking you."

Jacob quickly interrupted and said, "I know, buddy. We still had the old phone in the car. Hannah put it in a pocket and forgot all about it but we smashed it to pieces in Airlie Beach. We've only stopped for fuel since then."

Dhillion replied, "That's great, Jacob, but they haven't stopped there. They have a photo of you and are going from town to town until they find you. From the information I can see, I don't think they can go back to base without you. It seems they have arrived in Cairns and since you weren't in the smaller towns, they strongly believe that you are there. You need to lie low for a while until they move on."

Jacob dropped his head in dismay and said, "Why can't they just leave me alone?"

Then Dhillion said, "You are lucky that they don't have all of your new details, so you are okay for now. Kewarra Beach is not somewhere they would invest too much time looking around in, so please lie low and I will keep you updated. As soon as I know something, you will, and you need to do the same with me. Okay?"

Jacob replied, "I will, buddy, and thank you for telling me. I do want to hear stories of your shenanigans but right now I need to work out what to do. Take care, Dhillion, and thank you! I truly appreciate it!"

"No probs," Dhillion replied. "You stay low, stay safe and we will talk soon."

And with that, the phone call was over.

Jacob repeated to Hannah everything he had just learnt from Dhillion. When he had finished telling her he said, "I feel like we shouldn't go tomorrow now, hun. We should lie low."

But Hannah wanted none of Jacob's cautiousness, saying, "If we don't go, then they are already starting to control what we do again. Enough is enough. Seriously, it will be fine. We are going, Jacob."

He nodded, and the conversation ended there.

# Chapter 13

Jacob and Hannah woke up the following morning and found it to be a beautiful day, perfect for a day out.

As they were both getting ready during the morning Jacob couldn't shake this feeling in his stomach, but he couldn't tell whether it was from being excited in regard to the proposal, or whether it was that feeling of something bad to come.

He didn't say anything to Hannah, but just carried on and tried to ignore it.

They started packing up the SUV with all the essentials for a good day out – a picnic blanket, food and whatever they could think of – that they might need if they were to get stranded or just wanted to relax.

Their drive to Kuranda was no longer than thirty minutes up the Kennedy Highway, which made its way through dense rainforest. Just having the window down brought them the smell of freshness and relaxation. It was a wondrous place that Jacob and Hannah were finally seeing.

Once they arrived in Kuranda the first thing they noticed was the rustic look of the markets with a brick-paved walkway in between the shops. They wanted to do some spending at the markets and perhaps bring some souvenirs home with them. There were some really nice 'hippie-style' clothing shops, organic products, handcrafted products and jewellery shops. They decided to stop for lunch and coffee, and sat outside just chatting about their surroundings.

After Jacob and Hannah had finished their lunch and had had a brief walk around the markets, they saw a wooden sign shaped like an arrow with the word 'Lookout' carved into it.

It was pointing towards a narrow walkway through the dense forest. They followed the walkway, which eventually came to a set of stairs that seemed to go on and on. Jacob led the charge up the stairs as he was so excited about this place being the ideal setting to propose to Hannah.

Jacob was playing with the ring in his pocket when he reached the top of the lookout. He was in total awe of the beauty of the raging waterfall that would occasionally spray the tourists who viewed it. His concentration was so firmly fixed on this one thing that his sixth sense was stifled with regard to the imminent accident.

As Hannah was climbing the steps, which were damp from the waterfall spray, her foot slipped and she began to fall backwards. It was as if time had slowed down. Jacob only heard Hannah yell to him. He felt her desperation and fear faintly at first and then once it had grabbed his attention, it all became ear-piercing as he swung around and saw her begin to fall.

Jacob's smile vanished in an instant and his eyes widened as he went to try and save her, but she was just too far clear of him to get to in time. As she fell back on the steps she began to tumble. One particular step on the fall would be the fatal step where she broke her neck.

Jacob yelled, "Nooooo!" as he ran down the stairs towards her. "Stay with me, baby, stay with me!"

But there was no response from her. He sat there crying with her head lying softly in his lap. Some tourists came down to the lookout.

He yelled to them, "Get help! Quickly!" They ran off and called the ambulance.

Agents Tillerson and Greenwood heard the ambulance call over the radio, but made a decision not to follow it up since it was in a tourist area and was just an accident. Little did they know that this was their only chance to catch Jacob unaware and at a vulnerable time. They had no idea how serious the repercussions would be for them, for not following this up.

When the paramedics arrived they checked Hannah's vital signs and then informed Jacob that she was gone. His cry of pain and loss was enormous as they put her lifeless body on a stretcher and took her back to the ambulance, with Jacob walking right there next to her. Once she was loaded into the ambulance Jacob ran to his car and followed them to the hospital.

Once Jacob arrived at the hospital there were two police officers waiting for him who did not faze him in the least, this time. When they wanted to ask him questions about the accident he obliged because, after all, there was no malice here, just a heart-wrenching tragedy for Jacob – and Hannah, of course. After a couple of hours telling the story and answering questions Jacob said to them, "Please, just let me go home now. I need time to process all of this and at least grieve!"

The police officers agreed to let him go home, and said that they would resume the rest of the questioning another time. They really couldn't get much more out of him anyway.

Once Jacob arrived home he grabbed a beer, sat down at his dining room table and pulled out the ring in its box from his pocket – the ring that he was going to propose to Hannah with. In his despair he began to sip on his beer while nudging the little box with the ring around the table. He began saying things out loud to himself like, "Oh Hannah, baby,

I'm so sorry. This is my entire fault. I should have been firmer with you when I said that we shouldn't have gone."

But his sentences and their tone began to change slowly to, "If those fucking agents had never chased me down and put me into that simulation shit we would never have been here for this to happen!"

His voice was starting to become highly aggressive as he began deflecting his self-accusations and putting all the blame on the agents because now, in his mind, her death was on them.

# Chapter 14

The following day Jacob had to call Hannah's mother to tell her about what had happened to Hannah, but he found out that she already knew. The police had already informed her of Hannah's death.

Jacob was constantly crying and apologising to her, but she tried to stop him, and told him that it wasn't his fault.

She informed Jacob that the funeral service would be in four to five days. Jacob said, "I'm not sure if I can get through it. I miss her so much and to see her like that … I just don't know."

Hannah's mother replied, "Jacob, I will see you there. You need to call your friends and let them know what's going on as well. Hannah has told me so much about you all and that they were extremely close friends to her as well. She would want you all there and it may help you to cope a little better, with them there with you." Jacob agreed.

Jacob and Hannah's mother shared one more condolence and said their farewells, as Jacob had a few phone calls to make.

Jacob called Dhillion, Adrian and Evan straight away to let them all know the situation. They were understandably all upset by the news. Adrian happened to be in between fishing trips at this time but was due back at sea within a week, so he cancelled the next trip to stay for the funeral. They had all sensed that Jacob didn't sound quite right. After all, who would be? They had noticed his emotional rollercoaster from sad to angry and then back to sad, in their conversations. Dhillion had found out as much information as he could about the simulation work done to Jacob so he began syncing his main computers to his laptop before he left. He had a feeling that he might need it, if Jacob was too upset and needed him to stay. He believed that it was better to be safe than sorry.

Everyone packed for a lengthy stay with Jacob, just in case it was required. They all arrived a day early and spent the night before the proceedings at Jacob's. As they all sat having a beer together for the first time in a long time, they began to realise how truly angry Jacob was becoming and that his eyes were changing from bright blue to a shade darker. They all knew what was coming but decided to say nothing until after the funeral.

On the morning of the funeral they all dressed very conservative-ly – suits, black polished shoes and hair styles as good as they could get them – in respect for the way Hannah always appeared. They all went together in Jacob's SUV, as the town which Hannah's mother had chosen for the funeral was a couple of hours away. She had organised this so as not to attract attention from the police. Or especially, from the agents.

When they all arrived they met Hannah's mother and sisters in person for the first time. Everyone spoke very highly of Hannah. The funeral service was a beautiful one where tributes flowed as quickly as the tears did. However, Jacob was a different story. He just stood there, straight-faced, with no sign of emotion. It was as if he were trying to stay calm, yet what was going through his head was anything but calm. All he could think about was revenge for Hannah, and he was willing to go to the ends of the earth to find it.

Towards the end of the funeral he began thinking about why they were living in Kewarra Beach and why he was still being hunted by agents. "Agents!" he said under his breath. Adrian was right next to him and said quietly to Jacob, "What did you say?" and Jacob replied, "Agents! All of this is their fault."

Adrian said, "We will talk about it later."

Everyone was given a rose at the end of the funeral and one by one they all placed their rose on top of the coffin. Then, as Hannah's favourite song was playing, Jacob, Adrian, Dhillion and Evan all helped to carry the coffin to the hearse.

Jacob all of a sudden started to hear talking and grieving that was ear-piercingly loud. But when he looked around, squinting his eyes, no one was talking. Sure, they were crying – but there was no talking. Jacob shook his head from side to side as if to shake it off, and it worked. The loud ear-piercing chatter stopped.

There were tears streaming down people's faces as the coffin was placed into position and then everyone stood there watching it descend. They were supposed to go to the wake afterwards; however, Jacob didn't want to take part in that. He was emotionally exhausted and needed to go home to rest, bearing in mind that it was a two-hour drive home.

Adrian, Dhillion and Evan all travelled back to Jacob's place with Dhillion, not just because they only had the one car – they could have found their own way back – but because they didn't want to leave Jacob alone while he was in this unpredictable state of mind.

Once they got back to Jacob's house Evan asked Jacob, "Are you okay?"

"No, mate," Jacob replied, "I'm pretty far from okay. I need to sort these agents out. They have chased us for too long and we all know that they won't stop until they find me. Hannah is gone and I don't want anyone else to die, including myself. No more hiding and no more running."

"What do you need from us?" asked Adrian. "We have lost a great friend as well, Jacob, and we don't want to lose another."

Jacob replied, "Dhillion – I may need your expertise to identify, as narrowly as possible, where they are. It's a big place here. Adrian – I could use your strength, if it comes to blows with the agents. And Evan – you could be our driver. What do you guys think of that idea?"

All of them agreed straight away to help. Dhillion went to the fridge, grabbed four bottles of beer, placed them on the table and said, "You guys open these and I will get my laptop."

Evan cracked the beers open and passed them around, and by the time he had handed the last one out, Dhillion had already returned with his laptop.

"I have synced my computers from home to this laptop so I can use any screen at will, so we are all good on my part," said Dhillion.

While he was setting it up Jacob said to them all, "Something strange is happening to me, guys. First Hannah and I were at the beach and I heard a girl screaming for help, yet Hannah couldn't hear a thing. Then when we were loading her coffin into the hearse I heard loud chatter above the grieving so I looked around and no one was talking. It's beginning to freak me out a bit."

Evan said, "Are you serious? Man, I knew you had some freaky ability to avoid accidents but this is off the Richter scale. You hear people's thoughts?"

Jacob replied, "It sounds insane, I know, but it started happening up here in Cairns."

Adrian then said, "That's something you need to hone in on. It will be handy when we go to take on the agents. If you could control it, that is."

Jacob replied, "I will try every now and then to see if I can get control over it, but I won't tell you when because I don't want any pressure while I try."

Adrian nodded in an understanding fashion.

"I'm in! Let's get this show rolling," Dhillion said, as he entered the database he had hacked on his laptop. "First things first, then."

"Where are they?" Jacob asked.

As Dhillion was punching keys on his keyboard, Jacob had both of his hands tightly clutched around his beer bottle as he looked down at the table. He was trying to hear his friends' thoughts and would continue trying until he got it.

"Okay!" Dhillion said. "They are definitely still in Cairns. They are at a hotel called Cairns Royal Hotel, and it looks like they have been there for quite a while now."

Hearing this news, Jacob began to get a little bit emotional and he put his hand in his pocket, rubbing the encased engagement ring. He was full of anger, sadness and oddly a bit of happiness or relief that the agents were relatively nearby.

All of a sudden Jacob heard "I … we … them."

It was a broken sentence, but it was Adrian's voice. Jacob looked up but nobody had said a thing, so he looked straight at Adrian.

Adrian said, "What? Why are you looking at me like that?"

Jacob replied with a smile, "I just heard a broken sentence from you, and yet you weren't talking out loud."

Adrian's jaw dropped, as did Dhillion's and Evan's.

As Adrian got up from his chair he said to Jacob, "Stand up. Stand up and look me in the eyes. I will think of a conversation and I want you to answer my questions."

Jacob then said, "Come on, Adrian. It's still new to me."

As Adrian put his hand out to help Jacob stand up, he said, "I don't care, mate. Training has commenced and we need you to be able to control this."

Once Jacob was up he looked Adrian in the eye and Adrian began rattling questions off in his mind. Dhillion and Evan both had a sip of their beer, looking on with anticipation.

Adrian was asking simple questions such as, *How old are you?* and *Where do you live?* but Jacob couldn't hear anything. Adrian then said out loud, "Maybe try using your emotions. Think of Hannah. Think of the agents who might be the key to unlocking this door and getting some control over it."

Jacob then closed his eyes, put his hand in his pocket and began to rub the box that held the ring. He thought for a minute, then slowly opened his eyes, looking straight at Adrian.

Adrian then asked the first question: *Where do you live?*

Jacob's knees almost gave way, while he was clutching his ears.

"Kewarra Beach!" he replied. "It's so bloody loud!"

"Set your own volume," Adrian said. "Because no one whispers thoughts, Jacob."

Dhillion and Evan looked at each other in amazement as Jacob stood back up. Adrian then asked in his mind, *Who is chasing you right now?*

"No one. I'm chasing *them*, now!" Jacob exclaimed with a smile. Then Adrian thought, as he was looking at Jacob, *Don't worry. We will get them.*

Jacob said, "I freaking heard that, Adrian! You said, 'Don't worry. We will get them.'"

Jacob threw both of his hands in the air and said, "Okay, okay, guys. This is getting too full-on and I am absolutely stuffed – not to mention how weird this is getting as well. Can we continue tomorrow, please? It's 8.30 pm and I'm exhausted."

Everyone agreed so they all called it a night, in order to prepare to come back fresh in the morning to resume where they had left off.

# Chapter 15

Jacob lay in his bed for an hour or so, just staring at the ceiling, thinking of his beloved Hannah. And of his new capabilities, which he was still in disbelief over. An hour later, he drifted off to sleep, to wake the next morning reinvigorated and ready as ever.

As Jacob was making his coffee, Evan woke up. He walked straight up to Jacob and grabbed him by the arm.

"I know what we need to do today."

"What is it, mate?"

"We need to go to a public place where you can test this out and get more control."

Jacob nodded in agreement as he poured his coffee and said, "Good call, mate."

Jacob and Evan sat down and drank their coffee, discussing where to go for Jacob to practise. Adrian and Dhillion, woken by Jacob and Evan's murmurs, came out to make themselves a coffee as well. Jacob had just decided on the best spot to train so they could avoid any attention from any kind of law enforcement. The last thing they wanted was to alert the agents to their whereabouts.

Jacob turned to them and said, "Palm Cove, guys! That's where we could do the training. We could start on the pier where there will be plenty of fishermen. Then we could head to the strip of shops along the beach. It's always busy down there."

"Sounds great," said Dhillion. "Let me grab my laptop to check some things out before we go."

Jacob replied, "Take your time, and mate, it's only three beaches down from here, so it's quite close."

Adrian then asked Jacob, "How are you feeling today, mate? Did you sleep well?"

Jacob assured Adrian that he was feeling good and was keen to get out there and begin.

Dhillion came back with his laptop. He sat down with the laptop and his coffee at the table and said, "It seems that the agents will be preoccupied with an accident in the city of Cairns, so we should be clear of them today, guys."

While Dhillion sat there drinking his coffee he was secretly finding phone numbers and attempting to trace the agents' movements. Dhillion decided not to tell anyone about this yet because he didn't see the need. He preferred to keep his findings as a surprise for later, when they were required.

Once they were ready and Jacob had done the pat down of his pockets to make sure the ring was with him, they all jumped into the SUV. Soon they arrived at Palm Cove, where they parked right in front of the pier in the car park – just in case it became overwhelming for Jacob. That way, they could leave as quickly as possible.

As they all began walking down the pier Adrian said to Jacob, "Don't forget, mate, you need those emotions to hear it and control it."

Jacob replied, "I know, and I won't forget."

As Jacob passed a few people the loud broken sentences began, and as he went to clutch his ears Adrian grabbed his wrist and said, "No. You need to control the volume yourself. Holding your ears won't help you with this."

So Jacob slowly dropped his arms and began to hone in on the broken sentences.

"They are all talking at the same time!"

Evan replied, "Of course they are; they are merely thinking. Try to maybe look at a person or listen to one person's thoughts without the rest."

"Good call!" Jacob reached into his pocket and began rubbing the ring as he tried to listen to a little boy with his dad. Jacob could barely hear the boy's thoughts through everyone else's, but the more attention he gave to them, the dimmer the rest were. After a few minutes he had dimmed the others' thoughts to practically nothing and could just hear the boy's thoughts.

Jacob said to Adrian, Evan and Dhillion, "I think I've got it. It's just the boy now."

With this they all smiled at each other. As Jacob was listening to broken sentences he suddenly heard a full one: *This is the best day of my life, just sitting here fishing with Dad, and we have been catching fish too.*

Jacob quickly drew out from his thoughts and was happy for the young boy. Now he had found that he could turn the volume up and listen to anybody.

As Jacob looked around at different people, he was going in and out of people's thoughts at will – with absolutely no disruption from anyone else's thoughts. Jacob now had full control!

"Have you got it sussed yet?" asked Evan.

"Yep. I do," replied Jacob. "Let's go to the shops and see how much control over this I do have."

As they walked through the shops, sure enough, he was only hearing the person he had given his attention to. Jacob just began looking around in amazement at what was happening.

Dhillion asked, "Now – can you turn it off?"

Jacob replied, "Give me a sec." As he secretly stripped his emotions away, the voices slowly disappeared to nothing. Jacob turned around to the guys with a smile and said, "They are off! Adrian, you're right, mate. It's all about emotional control, and it varies from no one to everyone.

"I do think that I have control now! But I want you guys to know that I will never use this on *you*, now that I have control of it, unless it was a matter of life and death. I don't want to invade your personal space – and to be honest I don't want to risk scaring my mind with your filthy thoughts!"

Everyone had a chuckle at this. They decided to walk around the shops a bit more because it was all new to Adrian, Dhillion and Evan. They wanted to just take in the sights and maybe buy a souvenir for themselves.

After an hour or so they all grabbed a takeaway coffee each and then jumped back into the SUV to drive back to Jacob's house.

# Chapter 16

Once they arrived, Dhillion went straight to the room he was sleeping in, grabbed his laptop and brought it out to the dining room table to see if he could track Agents Tillerson and Greenwood. Evan stared at Dhillion and asked, "What are you up to? You seemed to be in an awful rush to get your laptop."

Dhillion then decided to tell everyone that he had found a way to track the agents.

Jacob turned to Dhillion and said, "Why didn't you tell us this earlier?"

"Well," Dhillion replied, "I wanted to tell you when you needed to know and now is that time. I think that we are good to go for tomorrow, if you are all keen to get this over with?"

Jacob said, "Yes. Let's do it. I'm sick of all of this. Can you send them a message without them knowing where it came from?"

Dhillion replied, "I think I could, although you need to give me a minute on that one."

While Dhillion was typing away on his laptop, Jacob pulled out the ring from his pocket, placed it on the table and said, "Guys, this is what has helped me channel my emotions."

"Please don't tell me that that's an engagement ring," said Adrian.

"Yes, mate," replied Jacob. "I haven't told anyone yet, but when Hannah died I was about thirty seconds away from asking her to marry me."

Adrian put his head down, shaking it slowly and said, "That sucks, mate."

Just as Adrian had finished the sentence Dhillion said, "Okay, Jacob, I think I'm ready. What message are we sending to these bastard agents?"

Jacob thought for a second and then said, "Okay, try this: 'I know you're here and I know you're looking for me but now I am after you and I don't need to look for you because I know where you are. I'm coming for you!' What do you guys think?"

Dhillion, Evan and Adrian all nodded in agreement. It was good enough to give the agents a bit of a jolt.

Agents Tillerson and Greenwood were out on a job when Agent Tillerson received the text message on his phone.

As he read it he said, "Well, well, well. Jacob *is* here, Greenwood. We were right to keep investigating up here and it seems that he will come straight to us."

Greenwood asked, "Is he turning himself in?"

Tillerson replied, "Unfortunately, no. He has decided to take it upon himself to attempt to attack us instead. He apparently knows where we are as well."

Greenwood replied, "We should be ready for him when he arrives."

"No need to be ready for anything," Tillerson said. "I highly doubt he has a gun. And it sounds like he is either by himself or possibly with one other."

Tillerson tried to send a message back to Jacob, but it just bounced back to him as 'Undelivered'. Tillerson found this interesting so he passed it on to home base in Melbourne for them to try and find out where Jacob's message had come from.

Jacob, Dhillion, Adrian and Evan all agreed that they would go after the agents the next day. Their intentions were not to kill them but to try to force them to back off and leave Jacob alone. However, Jacob knew that they would not back off that easily. They would chase him to the ends of the earth.

# Chapter 17

The following morning Jacob was making his coffee as usual when Adrian came out and said, "How are you this morning? I hope that you've got that sensational ring with you. We need her help today."

Jacob replied with a smile, "I'm good, mate – and yes, I always have it and her with me!"

Not long after Adrian and Jacob had woken up, Evan and Dhillion woke up. Dhillion had his laptop under his arm.

"Looks like you're all set for today," Adrian said with a smirk. Dhillion replied, "We have to be. I hope you all truly understand the dangers of today. The only weapons we have are my technology, Jacob's telepathic ability, Adrian's brawn and Evan's driving skills. I'm pretty sure that the agents will have guns, or tasers at the very least. This will be a dangerous mission today, guys."

Jacob replied, "Yep, you're right. So we should all know the dangers by now and if anyone wants to pull out, please say so. No one will think any less of you if you do want to pull out. So – does anyone want to stay here until we get back?"

Everyone shook their heads. Dhillion looked around the room and said, "Looks like we are all in it together. Let's get ready; we need everything to be ready to go at a moment's notice. I will have my laptop ready. Adrian – maybe you should work with Jacob to make sure you're good to go in that department."

Everyone agreed with Dhillion and so Adrian began training with Jacob.

Adrian would think of a sentence or question, and while Jacob was tuned in he would hear it clearly and would respond. Every now and then Jacob would burst out laughing at a joke Adrian had thought of.

Dhillion made sure his laptop was fully charged and in sync with his computers back home and had a tracking system operating constantly on the whereabouts of agents Tillerson and Greenwood.

Once everyone was ready, Jacob put on his Starter baseball cap and they all jumped into the SUV. Evan was driving, with Dhillion in the front passenger seat, while Jacob and Adrian sat in the back. Dhillion was directing Evan straight to the agents via the GPS on his laptop.

Agents Tillerson and Greenwood were still in their hotel sifting through paperwork, which is exactly where Dhillion had tracked them to. As they arrived Jacob said, "Evan, please wait here with the car in case we need a quick getaway. I have a feeling this may be a fifty-fifty situation. Dhillion, please track my phone so you know precisely where we are. And Adrian, let's do this."

As Adrian and Jacob left the car and began walking into the hotel, Jacob felt a massive shiver run through his body, but he ignored it and said, "I will sit at the bar, and perhaps you can sit on those chairs nearby as if you don't know me. They only know my face, mate, not yours."

Adrian replied, "Rightio, but I think I should be closer to the door."

Jacob agreed. As he walked up to the bar, he became awash with bad feelings of impending doom, but he would never leave or give up his chance of revenge for Hannah's death.

Jacob looked at the bar stools and decided that the stool at the end of the bar, but closest to the doorway that they had come in through, was the best one. It was also closer to Adrian, which gave Jacob some comfort. As he sat down he ordered a light beer, but as soon as he went to sip it his phone began to ring.

Jacob looked at the phone. It was Dhillion, so Jacob quickly answered it.

Dhillion said, "They are on their way down from the room, so make sure you're ready!"

Jacob replied, "Okay" and hung up, looked at Adrian and pointed down to the ground. Adrian knew what Jacob was trying to say so he just gave Jacob the thumbs up and sat at the edge of his seat, pretending to read the newspaper.

The agents walked in, discussing the last job that they had responded to. As they approached the bar, Tillerson saw the guy at the bar with the Starter cap on and thought, *Jacob*.

Jacob heard this thought. As Agent Tillerson walked past Jacob he said, "Jacob, you have balls coming here by yourself."

Just as the agent pulled out his handcuffs, Adrian sprang into action. With a vicious look on his face, he ran to Agent Greenwood and punched him square in the nose. Jacob spun around on his bar stool and kicked Agent Tillerson in the stomach, which made the agent keel over. Jacob grabbed Tillerson's hair and ploughed his knee straight into Tillerson's face. Then Jacob whispered into Agent Tillerson's ear, "It's over. Leave me alone."

But Tillerson replied, "Not by a long shot!" as he pulled out his gun and shot Jacob in the shoulder. Jacob screamed in pain. Adrian kicked the gun out of Tillerson's hand, picked Jacob up and ran for the door.

Adrian didn't realise that Agent Greenwood had a gun as well. While they were running to the door, shots were being fired at them. Just as they got outside the glass door, one of Greenwood's shots went straight into Jacob's back.

Jacob fell to the floor. As Adrian tried to drag Jacob to the car, Greenwood got another shot away, which caught the back of Adrian's knee and he dropped down next to Jacob.

Jacob was in so much pain, and going through such anger and sadness that he yelled out, for the last time, so loudly that a glass window exploded. The strange ear-piercing high-pitched sound had the agents rolling around in pain. It was Jacob keeping them away.

Jacob turned to Adrian as Dhillion and Evan were running towards them and said, "I'm not going to make it this time, mate."

Adrian replied, "Come on, Jacob. Stay with us, mate."

Jacob pulled out the ring from his pocket and passed it to Adrian.

"Look after this. It's a symbol of Hannah and me and whenever you look at it we will be with you."

Adrian pushed it back to Jacob and said, "No. This is for you two only."

As Jacob started to cough up blood he said to Adrian, Dhillion and Evan, "You are all great friends, and I will miss you forever. You have all meant the world to me. Now go! I have the agents incapacitated but I can't hold them there much longer. Get in the car and go now!"

They all did as he demanded. As Jacob watched them running to the car, everything he could see began to fade away into a tunnel surrounded by blackness. The tunnel became smaller and smaller, just as it had when he was at the warehouse.

At the end of each simulation this was what would happen.

Jacob whispered, "Oh, no!"

The tunnel became so small that it disappeared completely, until it was all darkness.

Jacob woke up back in the warehouse, still strapped to the chair with the simulation helmet on.

# PART 3:
# TIME AFTER TIME

# Chapter 18

J acob woke up in a dreamy state. He slowly realised that he was strapped to the chair, still with the simulation helmet on.

This time, Jacob recalled everything. As he had a brief look around at the massive windows in front of him, he slowly began to get angrier. He put his head down and looked at his lap, and noticed the ring bulging slightly from his pocket. Jacob began to breathe heavily and sweat profusely as he flashed back to everything he had been through and lost.

He slowly lifted his head and gave out an almighty cry. As he stared at the ceiling and yelled, the windows in front of him exploded, just as Hannah and Adrian were coming to his rescue once again.

Jacob only heard footsteps. He knew people were coming, and in his anger he had assumed the worst. He once again looked down at his lap and then looked straight ahead as his eyes faintly began to change colour.

Hannah and Adrian fell to their knees in excruciating pain as Jacob presented an ear-piercing high-pitched pulse to disable whoever it was that was in the vicinity. Hannah clutched her ears and said, "Jacob! It's … it's us!" Jacob slowly turned his head and as soon as he saw Hannah he stopped the noise immediately, giving a deep breath of relief.

"You're here!" he said. Hannah replied, "Of course we are and we are getting you out of here."

Both Adrian and Hannah began unstrapping Jacob.

"What the hell was that noise?" Adrian asked. "Did the agents rig something up here that we didn't know about?"

Jacob replied, "No. It was me. We've got a lot to talk about, but for now just get me the hell out of here and I will tell you soon enough."

Adrian and Hannah looked at each other with some confusion while they both helped Jacob up and out of the chair. As they were carrying him out, Hannah reached out to grab Jacob's mobile phone. Jacob noticed and quickly and loudly said, "*No!* Do not bring that. It will help them find us. Just leave it." Hannah put the phone back down again while looking at Jacob in confusion.

Jacob turned to Adrian and said, "It's great to see you again, my friend. We have been through a lot together. You won't remember a lot of what we have been through but I just wanted you to know that. And Hannah," he said, as he turned to her, "I love you so much and I will make sure that nothing happens to you this time around."

Hannah said, "This time around?" and Jacob replied, "The last time, you died right in front of me. That won't happen again, I promise you."

As they got closer to the car, Hannah was about to question Jacob when Evan rolled down his window and said, "Jacob! Quick! All of you get in the car. We have to go now!" As they were all getting into the car Evan took off as soon as the last person had sat down without even having time to close the door. With that, Dhillion said, "I have some bad news, Jacob. You have been trapped in a simulation."

Jacob cut Dhillion off straight away. With a wry smile he said, "I know, mate, I know, and we are still in one. It will all make sense soon. I understand that you think that you have saved me, which you have, but what you don't know is that this is the second time you have done it. Maybe more, if there are times that I don't remember." Jacob sighed and said, "I need a coffee."

Dhillion thought to himself, *He has become delusional. What have they given him?* He said out loud, "Jacob, we need to get you out of here. We will go to your place. I need you to collect as much stuff as you need."

Jacob was still a little dazed. He smiled and said, "Don't bother. We would end up going straight to your place after that anyway, so let's just skip my place. We are going to Dhillion's place."

Hannah was staring into Jacob's eyes as he spoke and realised that he may not be so crazy and that this might actually be real. She turned to Evan and said, "We are going to Dhillion's place. Step on it."

Once they had arrived at Dhillion's house, Jacob began to feel somewhat better and could walk himself to the door. As they all walked in, Jacob smiled and said, "Don't smell the flowers. Hannah did the same thing. They are fake."

Hannah's eyes opened wide. "How could you possibly know that? You weren't here then!" Jacob replied, "I told you, I've done this before, and please, Dhillion, I don't want a new identity this time. Please leave everything as it is. I want the agents to find me. Not to get back at them so much, but to talk to them and try to get some answers."

Adrian interrupted. "What the hell is going on? Please, mate, tell us!"

As Adrian was making the coffees, Jacob reached into his pocket and pulled out the ring in its box and placed it on the table. He opened the box to show the ring to his friends. They all gasped at it and as Adrian was walking over to the table with the coffees he opened his mouth in shock and said, looking at Hannah, "That looks like an engagement ring!"

Jacob lowered his head and said, "Yes, it was – until the accident."

"What accident?" Hannah asked.

Jacob replied, "I had bought this for you, Hannah, while we were living in Cairns. We went to Kuranda and had a fantastic day and I found the most perfect spot to propose to you. Unfortunately you were walking up the steps and you tripped and fell. I didn't sense it because I was so preoccupied with the excitement of the proposal that I couldn't save you. You died in front of me."

"Did you dream this?" Hannah asked. "We have never lived in Cairns, Jacob."

Jacob lightly tapped his hand on the table, pointed to the ring and said, "Then where did that come from? It was in my pocket when I woke up. This is exactly what I need to explain to you all. I think that we are in a loop of sorts. This is all playing out as it did before, except that I am changing a few things. Like the phone you tried to pick up, Hannah. Last time, that was what led the agents straight to us, because no one knew about it being in my jacket pocket in the back of the car. Adrian – at the end you got shot. And I died … which is what brought me to this rerun of what happened. Please don't get me wrong; I am so grateful and happy to see you all again. I just have to know exactly what's going on."

Evan said, "Okay. If that's what you want, then that's what we will do."

"How did you make that noise in our heads at the warehouse?" Adrian asked. "It was so freakin' loud!"

Jacob smiled and said, "I can do something else too."

"What is it?" Evan asked.

Jacob looked at Hannah and said, "Don't speak. Just think of a question or something you want to say and I will answer you."

Hannah looked at Jacob with curiosity and said, "Okay. Let's do it."

Everyone else was perplexed by what was going on in front of them. As Hannah looked into Jacob's eyes she began to think, *Did I really die?*

Jacob replied vocally with sad eyes, "Yes, you did."

Hannah then thought, *I am so sorry you had to go through that. It's not your fault. I hope you understand that.*

Jacob again replied vocally, "I did blame myself at first, but after the funeral I was full of rage and blamed the agents. I just wanted to get them and make them pay – which is what led to my death."

Hannah had tears streaming down her face and said quietly but verbally, "Holy shit."

Jacob replied with a smile, "Holy shit, indeed. I can switch this telepathic thing on and off at will but I made a promise to you all that I would not use it on you without your consent and I mean to keep that promise."

# Chapter 19

Meanwhile, outside of the simulation in the real world, a pair of ASIS agents named Jackson and Sacco were keeping an eye on the simulation.

Agent Sacco was the most enthusiastic about the simulation. He would watch it often, even at home, and on this occasion that's exactly where he was. Agent Sacco had hooked up his laptop to access the feed to the simulation on the big-screen television at home.

One night he was at the agency's headquarters watching the simulation when he noticed an anomaly with Jacob. He had never seen anything quite like it, which startled him. Agent Sacco jumped onto the phone straight away and called Agent Jackson. When Jackson answered the phone call he said, "This had better be an emergency, Sacco. It's one o'clock in the morning."

Agent Sacco replied, "Yes. It is an emergency. You know the simulation program that we are keeping an eye on? Well ... I think that there has been a serious glitch." Agent Jackson sat up on his bed rubbing his eyes and said, "What kind of glitch?"

Sacco replied, "I think that we need to meet at the office because it appears that there has been a restart problem. Jacob remembers the last simulation!"

"Oh, no. Okay, I will be there shortly. See you in thirty!"

Agent Jackson lent over and gave his wife a kiss, jumped out of bed and mumbled under his breath, "Bloody Sacco with his bloody simulation obsession."

Once he was dressed, he walked out the front door down to his car and set off. On his way he stopped off at McDonald's to buy a coffee for each of them. He knew there was no going back to bed tonight. If what Agent Sacco had said was true then it would be a long haul trying to work out what had happened.

When Agent Jackson arrived, he walked through the doorway and saw Agent Sacco sitting and staring at his computer screen in the dark, with his jaw dropped open, while shaking his head in disbelief.

Agent Jackson rolled his eyes and quietly said, "Oh my God, this is crazy." He switched on all the lights as he walked over to Sacco and said, "This had better be good. Your obsession with this thing will be the end of me."

Agent Sacco took the coffee from Jackson and said, "Sit down here."

As Agent Sacco began to pull out a chair next to him he continued with, "Seriously. Sit down here. This will blow your mind."

Agent Jackson sat down next to Sacco and said, "What is it?"

"Look!" Sacco pointed to the screen. "Jacob remembers everything from the previous simulation. Not only that, he brought an object from the last simulation with him. It's the ring he kept in his pocket."

Agent Jackson put his coffee down onto the desk, pulled himself closer to the screen and said, "That's impossible! How did this happen?"

"I don't know, but there must have been some kind of glitch, like I was telling you over the phone. Jacob still has his telepathic powers as well. This could seriously get out of hand quickly if he keeps pushing his limitations. Because as far as we know, there aren't any."

# Chapter 20

Agreeing with Sacco, Agent Jackson said, "We may need to bring in the specialist."

Agent Sacco replied, "Do you mean that scientist IT guy? The guy who created this whole program?"

"Hang on a minute." Agent Jackson shoved his hand into his pocket and pulled out his wallet. He flicked through his cards and pulled one out.

"Mr Ivan Stebhens!" Jackson exclaimed. "This is the guy we will be calling. We should probably do it now and not wait till morning. This has become an extremely bizarre situation and he is the only one, to my knowledge, who can help."

Agent Jackson quickly pulled out his phone and dialled the numbers on the card. It didn't take long for Mr Stebhens to answer and Agent Jackson gave him a rundown of what had happened as quickly as he could. Once Jackson was done explaining the situation Mr Stebhens said, "I told them that this was a dicey situation. To hook someone up to the system and transfer their consciousness is one thing. But to completely copy the consciousness so that the subject can just up and leave without knowing any better is entirely another. I always worried about the implications of a fully conscious and aware mind being completely copied into our simulation."

Agent Jackson asked Mr Stebhens, "Will you be coming down, then? This isn't the time to express personal views right now. We need to fix this issue." Mr Stebhens replied, "Yes, yes, yes. I am just getting my things together as we speak. I will be there as soon as I can."

Mr Stebhens arrived at the agency, a man with untidy frizzy brown hair, yet with very neat casual clothing. He walked straight to where Jackson and Sacco were sitting with the laptop, pulled up a chair and sat down beside them. Agent Sacco eyed Mr Stebhens's hair and clothing choice with a confused look and said, "Thanks for coming down." Mr Stebhens replied, "You're welcome. Now let's take a look, shall we?"

As Mr Stebhens grabbed the computer mouse he began to somehow rewind the simulation. Agent Sacco, having been so involved in the simulation, said, "I didn't know you could do that!" Mr Stebhens replied, "I created a few things in case some kind of an issue arose. From what I can see this is a huge problem and there are only two choices."

"What are they?" Agent Sacco asked.

Mr Stebhens replied, "We either pull the plug on the whole simulation or we let it carry on. However, if we were to let it carry on, Jacob could become even more powerful and hostile. I was not even aware that it could be possible for Jacob to remember the previous simulation after a reboot. He may have formed some kind of connection to the program. I just think that if his abilities keep growing, I don't know where they will stop. Especially given the fact that he has already done something that I thought to be impossible."

Jackson then said, "Obviously we all realise that he had some kind of telepathy or sixth sense before he was copied into the simulation, because that's why Agents Tillerson and Greenwood chose him, and then his friends, for this trial. So my question to you is this: Could it be possible for Jacob to grow his abilities here, just as his copy has done there?"

Mr Stebhens replied, "I'm sorry, Jackson, I don't have those answers. However, I highly doubt it. Within this simulation the consciousness is not as bound by laws as we are. For example, we do not have a reboot when we die. I have noticed, however, that none of the other subjects advance at all, when it comes to telepathy or physical strength."

Agent Sacco then leaned back in his chair with a shocked look and said, "Subjects? Aren't Jacob's friends just a memory of his that has been used in the simulation to depict them?"

Mr Stebhens replied, "No. All of his friends, and also the agents themselves that you have been watching, have had their consciousness copied. When Hannah, Dhillion, Adrian and Evan came to rescue Jacob we knew very well that they were coming. Dhillion is terrific with computers but we have better, fully trained people in this area. We seized them, when they tried to distract us, and we asked them to participate in the simulation. We told them that it would take no longer than ten minutes and that afterwards they would be released with Jacob. They would be well compensated as well, and would be allowed to go on to live their lives relatively quietly. Naturally they agreed."

Sacco, still leaning back in his chair with his mouth slightly open, said, "Wow! I had no idea that this much had happened. So now Jacob's copy in the simulation is in a loop, right?"

"Yes," Mr Stebhens replied. "Every time he dies, the simulation will restart. However, from now on he will remember what he wants and bring what he wants with him into the next simulation, as well. We seriously need to get to the warehouse right now."

"What for?" Jackson asked.

Mr Stebhens turned to Jackson and replied, "Well, I need to go into the simulation. I have created a setting where I can go in but I can also get out whenever I want, providing that someone is there to help. Leave the computers or laptops. There are plenty where we're going. And it's not too far from here."

Jackson and Sacco looked at each other. They shrugged their shoulders and Sacco said, "Okay, then. Let's go!"

# Chapter 21

In the meantime, at Dhillion's house within the simulation, Jacob was showing Hannah his telepathic abilities. Dhillion said, "I have an idea. What if we find the agents? They will be looking for us so we may as well let them find us."

Evan turned to Dhillion and said, "How do you suppose we do that?"

Dhillion replied, "The same way we busted Jacob out of that warehouse."

"Exactly," Jacob said. "Use your computers in your room to let them know via text message."

Hannah and Adrian both looked at each other in bewilderment, wondering how Jacob knew this. They were still finding it all hard to come to terms with.

Jacob sat at the table with a little smile, but he was feeling a little sad inside as he began to reflect on the loss of Hannah, before. At the same time he was feeling very grateful and lucky to have such great friends, knowing how far they would go for him.

Suddenly Adrian had a thought. He was thinking of Dhillion's computer equipment.

"Jacob," he said, "this is just an apparent recurring simulation, right?"

Jacob replied, "Yep."

Adrian then continued, "So we have nothing to lose. Why don't we just do what Dhillion said and bring them here to us?"

Dhillion swung around in shock and said, "Are you kidding me? Look at what I have here. They will lock me up for sure. Can't we go somewhere else? Maybe we could meet them in a public place."

Jacob jokingly said, "Okay, so firstly, we don't want you to be locked up. However, if you were, it would only be until I die, apparently. Secondly, I think going to a public place is a great idea. No police, no backup and plenty of people around; just us and them."

Adrian turned to Jacob and said, "How about where we met? I thought that they had great coffee at the Tram Stop Café and we haven't been there since the accident."

When Hannah heard this she said, "Yes, that's true, Adrian, but that was technically before the apparent simulation. In any case, I think that the Tram Stop Café is a great idea."

Evan said, "Well, Dhillion and I have never been there before, obviously because we met you afterwards. Let's do it. I'd like to see this place."

Now that they were all in agreement Dhillion said, "Okay, let me work my magic. And it would be great if I could have a coffee for this, or a Scotch – either way."

Hannah replied with a chuckle, "I can make you a coffee. I think it's a little early for Scotch."

"Okay," Dhillion replied. "Sounds good to me. What time do we want to meet the agents, guys?"

Jacob replied, "In two hours or so. Enough time for them to get there and also enough time for us. There is no point waiting any longer."

As Dhillion sat down in his computer room, Evan said to Jacob, "I hope they get back to us with a reply to the message."

Jacob responded, "They can't. It's untraceable and it can't be replied to. We just have to hope that they turn up."

As Hannah walked into the computer room with Dhillion's coffee, Dhillion said, "What would we like to say in the message?"

Jacob replied from the dining room table, "Just tell them to meet us there. No one else but those two agents. And make sure you let them know how many of us there are so they don't get spooked. This is a meeting to make a deal. I'm sure that that will entice them to come down."

Not five minutes later, Dhillion walked out of the room with his empty coffee mug, saying, "It's all done, guys. They will be receiving the message as we speak."

Jacob replied, "Good stuff, Dhil! Let's all head down there now. There is no point waiting around here and we are probably better off arriving there first to show our good intentions. It will hopefully be less of a shock for the agents as well if we are all sitting down."

Evan said, "You know that it will allow them to put a tracking device of some kind on the car if we get there first, Jacob?"

Jacob replied, "It doesn't matter, after this meeting, Evan. I have a strong feeling that this meeting is more important than we think. My senses are telling me that something much bigger will happen there."

"Like what, Jacob?" Hannah asked.

Jacob replied, "I don't know. But what I do know is that we have to leave right now."

Adrian then said, "Okay, then let's go. Everyone needs to get into the car. If Jacob says it's a big deal then it's a big deal. We need to be there first."

They all quickly walked out to the car and seamlessly everyone avoided the driver's seat as it had become expected that Evan would drive. Not that this worried him, though. He had always enjoyed driving because it gave him a sense of leadership and he also enjoyed just letting other people relax.

The Tram Stop Café was no more than fifteen minutes away, so once they had parked the car they all walked around the corner. When Jacob saw the café he said, "We should all sit outside."

He pointed to a table and chairs and said, "I will order takeaway coffees and bring them out to you. I will be back soon, guys."

With that, everyone sat down at the table that Jacob had pointed out and took in the nice street view as they waited patiently for his return.

# Chapter 22

Agents Tillerson and Greenwood had been waiting for quite some time for the meeting that had called them away from the warehouse, while keeping tabs on Jacob. They had finally come to the conclusion that it didn't exist at all.

On realising this, they quickly jumped into the car and headed back to the warehouse.

Tillerson said to Greenwood, "I hope Jacob hasn't been rescued. It will be hard to find him if he is gone. But if he is, I highly doubt that they would go back to Jacob's house, and if they have, you wouldn't think that it would be for long."

As Agents Tillerson and Greenwood arrived at the warehouse they both hastily got out of the car and ran inside to check on Jacob. As they got closer to where Jacob had been sitting, Agent Greenwood said, "Oh, dear God! Look at the windows, Tillerson. They have been completely blown outwards. There is not a single bit of glass on this side of the window at all! How is that even possible?"

Agent Tillerson replied calmly, "Maybe he has more power than we thought. We need to be careful here. Let's go to his house. I'm sure that they aren't there, but we may find clues. He didn't take his mobile phone, either. It's still sitting there on the table. It may very well be hard to track him down, so we had better get moving."

Agents Tillerson and Greenwood were just about to walk out of the warehouse when Tillerson heard a 'ding' from his pocket. He had received a text message on his phone. He reached into his pocket and pulled out his mobile phone. As he began reading the message he began to smile.

Greenwood said to Tillerson, "What's going on?" Tillerson handed the phone to Greenwood and said, "Read this! I can't believe it myself."

As Greenwood was reading through the message he said, "They are turning themselves in? What could be so important that he would walk straight back into the hands of the people who captured him?"

"Maybe they have worked something out, or maybe they want to ambush us," Tillerson replied. "However, they have picked a very public place so I don't think it would be the latter. I think that we should go and see what they have to say. We can put a tracker on their car, just in case things go south. What do you think, Greenwood?"

Agent Greenwood nodded in agreement and said, "Absolutely! Whatever we can do to make sure that they don't get away from us would be very helpful. Although I'm hoping that they might have a good deal for us as well. We should get going, then."

Agent Tillerson agreed, as he gave one last glance around the warehouse, and began walking away towards the car with Greenwood.

After thirty minutes' drive, Agents Tillerson and Greenwood arrived near the Tram Stop Café and decided to park around the corner so that they wouldn't be seen by Jacob and his entourage. The agents had spotted their car not far from their own so Tillerson opened his glove box and pulled out the small device that they would use for this exact situation.

Agent Tillerson pressed the back of the device, which was no bigger than a human thumb, and it lit up red. Greenwood opened an application on his mobile phone that would sync with the tracking device. The application began to search for the device and then once it was found, it automatically locked on to its whereabouts.

"It's ready," Agent Greenwood said. Agent Tillerson replied, "Good. Put it under the rear bumper of their car as we walk past."

Greenwood nodded as he and Tillerson stepped out of the car and began their short walk to the Tram Stop Café, where Greenwood did as instructed. When they were passing the car he knelt down and attached the device under the rear end. He then quickly went back into stride, walking alongside Tillerson.

As Tillerson and Greenwood came around the corner and into sight of the others, Hannah was the one facing in their direction. Hannah saw the two suits headed their way and said to the others, "Here they come. Two suits, and they look like they are alone."

Dhillion said to Hannah, "Don't forget that they have no idea what we look like. They only know Jacob."

It was nearly perfectly timed as Jacob walked out of the café with their takeaway coffees in a holder while the two agents approached.

"Jacob," Tillerson said, "we meet again. Good job on the window by the way."

Jacob placed the coffees on the table. He turned his head to the agents with a little smile and said, "Thank you. I thought it was a fantastic job myself but I think that we have more pressing issues to discuss, don't you?"

Tillerson replied, "Indeed. To kick it off we would like to hear what you have to say and then we can go from there."

As Greenwood nodded in agreement, Jacob said, "Please, have a seat with us. This is a safe place, for our part, and I have a lot to tell you."

As the agents sat down at the table, Jacob began to explain how they were all part of the simulation and that this was the second time he had been through it, as far as he could recall. He then pulled out his ring and explained as much as he could.

# Chapter 23

Meanwhile, outside of the simulation, Agents Jackson and Sacco were driving Mr Stebhens to the warehouse so that he could insert himself into the simulation for a brief time.

As they pulled up at the warehouse, Agent Sacco said, "I'm actually excited to see this setup in the warehouse with my own eyes." Mr Stebhens stepped out of the car. "It will blow your mind," he said.

As they were walking up to the warehouse, Agent Jackson asked, "What exactly is your intention when you go into the simulation?"

Mr Stebhens replied, "Well … like I told you, I will give them the two choices. But before that, I will give them a crash course on what is really happening. Once the choice has been made you will need to bring me out of the simulation. I will explain that to you in a minute."

Mr Stebhens then opened the door to the warehouse. As they all walked in, Agent Sacco gasped and said softly, "What the … ?"

Mr Stebhens said to them, "Yes. It's something, isn't it? Come over here!" He pointed to the chair. "I will put this helmet on and then I need you to help strap me into the chair."

Agent Jackson asked, "Why are we strapping you into it? It's not like you're a flight risk or anything."

"It's not for capture, it's for safety," Stebhens replied. "The subject sitting in this chair will wake up disoriented, and so I need to remain strapped in for a minute, after I wake up."

Mr Stebhens turned on the computer next to the chair, and as he began putting the strange helmet on his head he said, "That computer will automatically sync with the rest, so you will be able to see the simulation. It will ask if you are 'Ready To Copy Subject'. Click 'No'. Then it will ask if you are 'Ready To Insert' and I want you to click 'Yes' on this one. I have set up the system as easily as possible, so that when I say that I am ready to come back, all you have to do is press the 'Escape' button on the keyboard, there. Agent Sacco, please open the third drawer."

As Agent Sacco opened the third drawer he said, "Okay, so I have a heap of syringes with what looks like a serum in them."

Mr Stebhens said, "Yes. Pick the one with the least amount." Sacco found the correct syringe and handed it to Agent Jackson. Agent Jackson then placed it onto the table and strapped Mr Stebhens into the chair.

Mr Stebhens said, "You need to inject it straight into the bloodstream. I'm sure that you have had blood taken before? It's the same deal here, except we are putting it in – not taking it out."

Agent Jackson nodded to Mr Stebhens as he was screwing the needle onto the syringe. "We will see you when you get back. Good luck with your talk in there. We will be watching and waiting anxiously for your return." Just as Agent Jackson finished his sentence he injected Mr Stebhens with the serum. Mr Stebhens quickly became drowsy and within twenty seconds he was asleep.

At first, the computer screen was showing his vital signs, but suddenly the screen changed to the question, 'Ready To Copy Subject' and Agent Sacco pressed 'No'. Suddenly another question appeared – 'Ready To Insert' – and Agent Sacco clicked 'Yes'. All of a sudden the simulation appeared on the screen. After Agent Sacco had clicked 'Yes', Mr Stebhens could see a faint dot of light that grew larger and larger extremely quickly, until it completely surrounded him and he suddenly appeared, standing next to the table where Jacob and the others were sitting.

# Chapter 24

Hannah was startled by the seemingly impossible appearance of Mr Stebhens.

"Where the hell did you come from? How did you do that?" She turned to everyone at the table and said, "This guy just appeared out of thin air!"

Everyone at the table turned to look at this man who had appeared from nothing, just as Mr Stebhens answered one of Hannah's questions quite bluntly. "I'm not from here. However, we do need to talk."

Jacob gave a sigh and said, "I had a feeling something this strange might happen. You're from outside of our world aren't you – outside of the simulation?"

"Yes, Jacob," replied Mr Stebhens. "Not only am I from the outside, but I suppose I am also the creator of this place."

Adrian dropped his teaspoon on the table, startling not only himself but everyone else. "I'm sorry," he said, "this is all so warped to me."

"I imagine that it would be, for you," Mr Stebhens replied. "Please, may I sit down and explain what's going on and why I am here?"

Agent Tillerson quickly grabbed a chair from the table next to him and swung around. "Please have a seat and tell us what in God's name is happening here."

As Mr Stebhens sat down nodding his head in agreement, he asked Evan, who was sitting right beside him, if he could try some of his coffee. Evan did not hesitate to say yes. As Mr Stebhens accepted the coffee from Evan he said, "I'm not here long but I would like to see how it tastes."

Evan replied, "That's fine, but please don't drink it all. I like the coffee here."

Once Mr Stebhens had drunk some of the coffee he handed it back to Evan and said, "It tastes so real here."

Everyone looked at him in confusion. Jacob decided to use his thoughts to communicate with Mr Stebhens: *That's enough! Tell us why you are here!*

With that, Mr Stebhens replied, "Wooow! Your abilities are amazing, but you are right; let's get to it."

Agents Tillerson and Greenwood looked at each other in confusion as Mr Stebhens went on to say, "The reason why I am here is that there has been a glitch in the simulation reboot. Jacob, when you died, it should have restarted as it usually does, but this time you brought not only your memory of the last simulation back with you, but also an object. By an object, I mean the ring."

Jacob then interrupted and said, "What do you mean by 'it should have restarted as usual'?" Mr Stebhens replied, "Well you think this is the second time, yes? Or maybe a couple more than that? Well, it's actually number two thousand five hundred and sixty-four. It was built to continue rolling from one simulation to the next, every time you die, without either you or anyone else being aware of it."

Jacob then asked, "Why are you doing this?"

Mr Stebhens replied, "It was created to study a mind like Jacob's to see what abilities can come of it. We had Jacob hooked up to the chair with the helmet on to copy his consciousness when his friends came to try and bust him out. We knew that they were coming and so we caught them and struck a deal with them: Allow us to copy your conscious minds as well and we will let you all free, including Jacob. It was a no-brainer for them, really. They got to be free with Jacob and to have normal lives, without interruption from us. Although I must tell you that this was a long time ago. I'm sorry, but this is all true. You are all merely copies of your original selves."

They were all horrified of the news. Adrian began to get agitated as Hannah kept as calm as she could to find out more information. She said, "But it seems as though our deaths don't trigger the reboot, like Jacob's."

Mr Stebhens replied, "That's correct. Jacob's consciousness is the major one. It's the switch to restart the simulation."

Adrian then asked, "What about these two?" as he pointed to the agents angrily.

Mr Stebhens said, "Yes. They are copies from the original subjects as well. We needed real agents' minds so that they could be unpredictable. We didn't want it to be easy for either you or Jacob."

Mr Stebhens noticed Jacob beginning to slowly clench one fist. He saw this as a slight show of internal aggression so he quickly decided to give them their choices.

"So, here it is. These are your choices: either we pull the plug on the simulation and end all of your lives or we leave the simulation running. However, Jacob needs to give me his word that he will not advance his powers beyond those he has now. Then you can all lead a seemingly normal life and grow old."

Hannah grabbed Jacob's hand and said, "Yes, we can do that. We would like to live out our lives."

Jacob added, "I give you my word. I will just live a happy normal-as-possible life with my friends." Everyone nodded in agreement and so Mr Stebhens stood up and said, "Right, we are all on the same page then. I will get right onto your request."

Mr Stebhens looked straight up and said, "Pull me out, guys."

Agent Sacco pressed the 'Escape' button and everything began to disappear into a circle while Mr Stebhens was exiting the simulation. The circle became smaller and smaller before it was completely gone.

As Stebhens began to wake up, Agent Jackson asked, "Are you okay?"

"Pull the plug," Mr Stebhens replied.

"But you promised them that they could live peaceful lives!" the agent protested.

Mr Stebhens explained. "Jacob was getting angry. He won't stop because I don't think he knows how to stop. He will get out of control. Go to the power box of the whole building and switch it off. Now!"

Agent Jackson did as he was told. He walked outside the warehouse, found the power box and flicked the switch to 'Off'. All the computer buzzing sounds began to fade away in the warehouse while inside the simulation, Jacob saw his whole world begin to drift away. It turned into a circle that got smaller and smaller as he yelled, "Nooooooo!" until there was complete darkness.

Mr Stebhens then said to the agents, "Let's go. Our job is done here and the problem has been fixed."

As they were exiting the building, they all looked back once more before closing the warehouse door behind them.

Printed in Great Britain
by Amazon